Miss Pickerell Goes on a Dig

Also by Ellen MacGregor
MISS PICKERELL GOES TO MARS
MISS PICKERELL AND THE GEIGER COUNTER
MISS PICKERELL GOES UNDERSEA
MISS PICKERELL GOES TO THE ARCTIC

By Ellen MacGregor and Dora Pantell
MISS PICKERELL ON THE MOON

MISS PICKERELL
GOES ON A DIG

by Ellen MacGregor and Dora Pantell

Illustrated by Charles Geer

McGRAW-HILL BOOK COMPANY
NEW YORK   TORONTO   LONDON   SYDNEY

All characters in this book are entirely fictitious.

Contents

1. The Mysterious Stranger 9
2. The Professor 21
3. Race Against the Bulldozer 30
4. An Important Assignment 40
5. "Stop at Once!" 49
6. The Governor Helps 58
7. Curious Objects 65
8. Record-Keeping and Rain 75
9. Down to the Indians 84
10. Cave-In 92
11. A Sign from the Rescuers 99
12. "Light, We Need Light!" 105
13. A Clue to the Past 110
14. Testing 116
15. Honorary Indians 121

Miss Pickerell Goes on a Dig

Mr. Gilhuly leaned out of his truck

CHAPTER ONE

The Mysterious Stranger

Miss Pickerell clapped her black hat firmly on her head, looked in her wardrobe mirror to make sure the hat was on straight, and stopping only to grab up her knitting bag with her keys and extra pair of glasses in it, ran quickly out of the house. She knew she was not being very polite. But she simply could not stay in the house another minute and listen to her oldest niece, Rosemary, practice the piano. Rosemary never took her foot off the pedal when she played. No wonder, Miss Pickerell thought, Rosemary's own piano had broken down and she had had to come and stay with Miss Pickerell while it was being fixed. Rosemary's father, who was also Miss Pickerell's brother, felt very proud of Rosemary's progress on the piano. He was very upset when the piano keys refused to move just as the summer vacation was beginning. Summer was the time for more practice than ever, he told Miss Pickerell, when he deposited Rosemary and her valise full of clothes and her briefcase bulging with music books at the Square Toe farmhouse on Monday.

And this was Friday. Miss Pickerell sighed and tucked a loose hairpin into place. She wondered where she ought to go this morning. She had no particular errands to do. A drive would be nice, she decided. She would settle her beloved cow and Pumpkins, her new black cat with the big yellow eyes, in the little red trailer attached to her car, and go off some place where it was quiet. Miss Pickerell always took her animals along when she went out in her automobile. They enjoyed the change. And they were very good company for her.

From where she was standing near the tomato plants that bordered her gate, Miss Pickerell could hear young Mr. Gilhuly's Rural Free Delivery truck climbing up the mountain. He would be on the private road that led up to Square Toe Farm in just about a minute. Miss Pickerell thought she should go and see if she had any mail.

Mr. Gilhuly leaned out of his truck when he saw her coming. He had red hair, a light-blue uniform cap that sat on the top of his head, and a very friendly smile.

"Nothing for you today, Miss Pickerell," he

called out. "It's a nice morning, isn't it? Nice and cool."

Miss Pickerell agreed that it was unusually cool for July.

"Got your seven nieces and nephews staying with you, I suppose," Mr Gilhuly went on, as he listened to the sounds coming out of Miss Pickerell's front-parlor windows. "Got them with you for the summer holidays, I guess."

"Only one of them is with me, Mr. Gilhuly," Miss Pickerell replied decisively. "And she's not here for the summer. She'll go home just as soon as her piano comes back from the repair place."

Mr. Gilhuly tapped the pencil he held in his hand against his steering wheel in time to the scales Rosemary was playing. "Doing them kind of fast, isn't she?" he asked Miss Pickerell.

"As fast as she possibly can," Miss Pickerell replied. "So that she can turn on the phonograph and listen to rock-and-roll records."

Mr. Gilhuly laughed out loud.

Miss Pickerell did not laugh. She did not think it was funny.

Rosemary finished the scale she was playing with a particularly loud flourish. Mr. Gilhuly and Miss Pickerell heard her slam the exercise book shut. Then came the screech of the phonograph being turned on too suddenly, and the unmistakable beat of the rock-and-roll music began.

"Got one more stop to make," Mr. Gilhuly said quickly, stepping on the gas and disappearing behind a curve in the road.

Miss Pickerell started to walk down the lane that led to her tidy red barn and to the fenced-in cow pasture beyond it. "I never thought I'd live to see the day," she said to herself, as she put her hands over her ears to block out some of the sound, "when I'd want to hear scales practiced on my piano. Why even with the pedal on full force, they're better than this . . . this . . ."

Miss Pickerell moved toward her barn as fast as she could. She kept her car with the little red trailer inside the barn. The trailer had a canvas awning over it to protect the cow against bad weather. Miss Pickerell got into her car and drove it down to the clover fields where her cow was grazing quietly. The cow seemed happy to see Miss Pickerell, who patted her affectionately and led her into the trailer.

Next, Miss Pickerell went to look for Pumpkins. She found him under an apple tree, all curled up in an old paper bag he had dragged

12

out of the kitchen. Miss Pickerell picked him up, carried him to the trailer, and placed him next to her cow.

As she started the car, Miss Pickerell thought she heard the telephone ringing. She debated with herself about turning back, but decided against it. Rosemary would eventually answer. She always did. And these days, most of the calls were for her anyhow, Miss Pickerell reasoned.

Miss Pickerell drove slowly along the twisted, shaded road that descended into the valley. The day was getting hotter. She wondered whether she ought not to go on to Square Toe City and stop off at the air-conditioned drugstore for an ice cream soda. Perhaps Mr. Esticott would be behind the soda fountain. When he wasn't acting as Square Toe City's baggage master, he worked part time at the drugstore. Mr. Esticott made ice cream sodas with Miss Pickerell's favorite peppermint ice cream. Her mouth watered at the very thought of it.

She proceeded toward the filling station that marked the turn-off point to the highway. The boy at the gas pump waved to her as she approached. Then he ran into the office and another younger boy came out. The second boy cupped his hands to make a megaphone and called, "Miss Pickerell! Miss Pickerell!" But she was now concentrating on getting her car and the trailer onto the highway. That was much more important, she thought, than anything the boy could possibly have to tell her. She did not stop.

"I'll be here later," she called back, as she slowly and carefully steered the car into the right-hand lane and settled herself down to enjoying the drive. She could guess what the boy wanted to say to her. He was a friend of Euphus, her middle nephew. Euphus and his friends always had questions to ask her about the trips she had made to Mars and the moon. They constantly begged to see her famous rock collection, too. Miss Pickerell was very proud of her rock collection. She did not mind letting Euphus and his friends look at it and exclaim over it, provided they talked one at a time.

Miss Pickerell kept her eyes on the road and her hands tight on the wheel as she drove. Traffic was beginning to get heavier. Cars whizzed by her, one after another. A new, shining, olive-colored bus, with PERFECT DAY-CAMP COMPANY printed in large orange letters along its side, passed much too close to her. The driver

14

shouted what sounded like a jumble of words through his rolled-down window. Miss Pickerell frowned.

"That kind of driving comes dangerously near to breaking the law," she remarked disapprovingly, while she took a quick look at Pumpkins and her cow to make certain they had not been alarmed. "And the very least that driver could have done, if he had anything to say to me, was to speak more distinctly."

Miss Pickerell was still thinking about the bus driver when she suddenly noticed the sheriff's black-and-white striped sedan, with its long, spindly antenna, reflected in her rear-view mirror. The sheriff, a tall, thin man who wore a big, silver badge on his jacket, motioned for her to move over to the side. Miss Pickerell did so immediately. The sheriff followed.

"Good morning, Miss Pickerell," he said. "I'm sorry I had to stop you, but you . . ."

The sheriff never finished what he started to say. The word "attention," repeated several times and followed by names and street numbers which were also repeated, came sounding in over his police radio. He scribbled a few notes on a pad that he took out of the dashboard compartment, said a hasty "excuse me" to Miss

Pickerell, and drove off with his siren screeching.

Miss Pickerell was both angry and mystified. It seemed to her that the sheriff really had no right to break off in the middle of a sentence that way. At the most, it would have taken him only a second to give her a hint. And what *was* it he had been wanting to tell her? "I can't possibly imagine," she declared. "And I'm not going to worry about it either."

Then, unexpectedly, a number of terrible questions came into her head. What had the bus driver been trying to tell her? And Euphus' friend, down at the gas station? Was it all the same thing? Was it something to do with her animals? Something she had not noticed?

She got out of the car instantly and looked each animal over from head to tail. Her cow had leaned way out over the back of the trailer and was munching some wild sweet grass that grew tall at the edge of the road. Pumpkins was sniffing the fresh air and the sunshine and purring contentedly.

Miss Pickerell breathed a sigh of relief and slid in behind her wheel again. She stepped on the starter and steered her car back onto the road. She was almost halfway to Square Toe

16

City by now. Traffic was much heavier and the
advertising signs were beginning to appear. A
bright green sign in the shape of a semicircle
carried the words: ONE MILE TO SQUARE TOE
COUNTY DINER, owner, M. RUGBY, formerly
with ASTRAL CAFETERIA ON THE MOON. Just a little farther on, the same kind of sign announced:
ONE-HALF MILE TO SQUARE TOE COUNTY DINER.
MOONBURGERS OUR SPECIALTY. And, at the fork
in the road that led into Main Street on the right-
hand side and out toward Square Toe River on
the left, Miss Pickerell saw a third sign which

read: FIVE HUNDRED FEET TO SQUARE TOE COUNTY DINER. FREE cup of coffee on FULL MOON NIGHTS.

Miss Pickerell burst out laughing when she thought of Mr. Rugby. She was feeling better already. Mr. Rugby always cheered her up. He was so pleasant and chatty, and she only had to half-listen as he rattled on enthusiastically from one subject to another.

"That's where I'll go," she decided. "I'll go and have a refreshing glass of iced tea and a visit with Mr. Rugby."

She pulled up alongside Mr. Rugby's diner and parked lengthwise so that she could keep an eye on Pumpkins and her cow through the window.

Mr. Rugby, his face rounder than ever under his starched chef's hat, his cheeks pink with excitement, ran out of the diner to greet her. He nearly tripped over his apron, which was much too long for him, as he helped her up the high step to the green screen door.

"Miss Pickerell," he asked breathlessly, while they were still standing outside, "where have you been?"

He did not wait for her to answer. "I tried to call you on the telephone," he went on, talking very fast. "Rosemary said you'd just gone

18

down the road in your car. I left a message for you at the gas station. Then I telephoned the Perfect Day-Camp. I knew their bus was scheduled to come down into the valley. And to make absolutely sure of reaching you, I called the sheriff and asked him to help me find you."

"Oh!" Miss Pickerell said. She understood at last about all the shouting on the road. And she certainly admired Mr. Rugby's thoroughness. But he still hadn't told her why he wanted to see her. She was just about to ask him this when he began to explain.

"Listen, Miss Pickerell," he whispered, as he led her inside. "The strangest customer came into the diner this morning. He's been sitting here for hours, eating one Eclipse Special after another. You remember my Eclipse Specials in the Astral Cafeteria, don't you, Miss Pickerell?"

"Yes, yes," Miss Pickerell said impatiently. "With the spongecake and the ice cream."

"He has with him the oddest-looking rock I've ever seen," Mr. Rugby continued. "You must see the queer markings on it. And he never lets go of the rock, even when he goes into the phone booth. He's called one long-distance number seven times. I heard him asking the operator to connect him every time, just before he closed the door. Once, he nearly closed the door in my face. It's all too mysterious to suit me, Miss Pickerell. Who do you think that man is?"

Miss Pickerell followed Mr. Rugby's gaze across the diner to the table in the far corner. She adjusted her glasses, peered intently, and replied, "I have a very good idea."

CHAPTER TWO

The Professor

It was hard to stand up in the very narrow space between the seat and the table of the corner booth. But the vigorous-looking man with the bushy eyebrows and the short gray mustache managed to do this when Miss Pickerell and Mr. Rugby approached him.

"Good morning," he said politely.

"Good morning," Miss Pickerell replied. "Please excuse me for interrupting your breakfast."

"Not at all," the man said, glancing down at the empty ice cream dishes in front of him. "I'm glad you call it breakfast. Most people wouldn't be so kind."

Miss Pickerell laughed. She had an idea she was going to like this man. He was so unexpectedly lively and friendly.

"I came over to tell you," she explained, "that I thought I recognized you. But now that I've heard your voice, I'm sure of it. I've watched you on television many times. And I've been reading all about you and your archeologi-

21

cal expeditions in the newspapers, Professor Tuttle."

She said the last two words quite loudly while looking significantly at Mr. Rugby. He began, in a sudden burst of energy, to clear off the table.

Then she remembered that she had not introduced either herself or Mr. Rugby.

"I'm Miss Lavinia Pickerell, Professor Tuttle," she said. "And this is my friend, Mr. Rugby."

"Mr. Rugby and I have already met," Professor Tuttle replied, "over his irresistible Eclipse Specials. Shall we have another now, Miss Pickerell? To celebrate our meeting? I've been looking forward for a long time to making your acquaintance. Your rock collection and your trip to the moon have made news, you know. Please sit down."

Miss Pickerell sat down opposite Professor Tuttle. Mr. Rugby, positively beaming with pride, ran off to get more Eclipse Specials. Professor Tuttle carefully moved his rock from the corner of the table to the seat beside him.

"Perhaps I should mention," he said, as he noticed three dishes which Mr. Rugby, in his haste, had forgotten to take with him, "that I eat so much only when I'm upset. On my arrival in

22

Square Toe City this morning, the station master told me there would be an unscheduled delay of four hours between trains. I've been making telephone calls ever since. At the state capital, where I'm expected, there is no answer. And the one man I know in this part of the state can't be reached. His office phone is constantly busy."

Miss Pickerell agreed that these experiences could be very annoying.

"Well," the professor went on, changing the subject. "Let's talk about your adventures, Miss Pickerell. Do you have any new ones in mind for this summer?"

"Not that I know of," Miss Pickerell replied, smiling and thinking how almost all the exciting things she had done had come about quite accidentally. "But I read on the science page of the Sunday newspaper about some new archeological site-spotting that you are intending to do. From the sky!"

"Do you mean the aerial reconnaissance, Miss Pickerell?" Professor Tuttle asked. "That's not really new. Archeologists have been doing it for years. We go up in a plane and survey the ground for good places to dig."

Miss Pickerell reflected about this for a second. She didn't think the idea sounded very practical. "It seems rather odd to me, Professor," she said, "to go up to the sky and look down from there when what you're looking for is under the ground."

Professor Tuttle chuckled. "Not odd at all, Miss Pickerell," he said. "From the air, we are able to detect soil patches and colors which frequently go unnoticed on the ground, sometimes by the very people who are walking right on them. Varied soil colorations can be evidences of buried buildings and lost cities that are hidden far below the surface."

Miss Pickerell thought this a most interesting consideration. "Is it also possible," she asked, "to determine from the surface soil whether there are any unusual rocks in the earth below?"

Professor Tuttle had never heard of such a method. "But talking about rocks," he said, "you might want to see this one I have with me. It's an important find, I think."

Mr. Rugby, just about to put two especially tall Eclipse Specials in front of Miss Pickerell and Professor Tuttle, stopped short. The professor went right on talking.

"I don't know what I did with the gray flannel wrapping I had this in originally," he said, as he lifted the rock to the table. "It probably doesn't matter, though." He carefully placed the rock between the Eclipse Specials that Mr. Rugby was setting down. It weighed about ten pounds, was almost as smooth as a cobblestone, and had a crusting of dirt over all its surface.

"Now, just take a look at these markings," the professor directed, pointing to the patterned lines he was tracing with his finger on one side of the rock. "They're very old. And much too regular, it seems to me, to be accidental. If they are man-made, as I suspect, they may be clues to the lives of people who inhabited this earth centuries ago."

Miss Pickerell put on her reading glasses to examine the rock more closely.

"And look, too," the professor continued, "at the regular ridges and the hollowed-out center. Human hands must have shaped those."

Mr. Rugby stared, open-mouthed.

Miss Pickerell commented that she had never thought about rocks from this particular point of view before. She made a mental note to herself to be sure to read the entire section about archeology in her encyclopedia that very afternoon. She hoped that Rosemary would have finished practicing or talking on the telephone by then and that the house would be quiet.

Professor Tuttle turned his attention to

spooning up ice cream. "What a pity," he remarked, when he finished the double scoop Mr. Rugby had served him and was just about to start on the spongecake underneath, "that I can't locate Mr. Humwhistel. He would so much enjoy seeing this rock."

Miss Pickerell looked unbelievingly at Professor Tuttle. "But I know Mr. Humwhistel," she said. "He's one of my very best friends."

"That's the man I'm looking for," Professor Tuttle exclaimed excitedly. "The one whose office . . . ."

"He's with the Boy Scouts," Miss Pickerell interrupted promptly. "He goes out with them every morning during the summer. Lately, he's been taking the Girl Scouts, too."

Professor Tuttle seemed a bit surprised. "Are we talking about the same Mr. Humwhistel?" he asked. "The man I know is a scientist."

"Yes," Miss Pickerell said. "And he loves teaching science to children. That's why he takes them on . . ."

"Excuse me," Professor Tuttle broke in, looking at his watch. "I don't have very much time. Would it be hoping for too much to think that either of you might know where I could find Mr. Humwhistel right at this moment?"

"Of course, we know," Miss Pickerell replied. "He's down near Square Toe River, past the intersection that leads from the bridge."

"I know a short cut. I can draw you a diagram," said Mr. Rugby.

"I'll take the professor," Miss Pickerell suggested quickly. She knew from experience all about Mr. Rugby's complicated short cuts. "I'd like to say hello to Mr. Humwhistel, anyway. Why don't you let Mr. Rugby take care of your rock, Professor Tuttle? You can bring Mr. Humwhistel back here to see it."

They left in her car. The ride was a brief one. Professor Tuttle had hardly finished complimenting Miss Pickerell on her ingenious idea for the trailer, when they arrived at the steep slope overlooking the river.

Miss Pickerell called out, "Yoo Hoo, Mr. Humwhistel!"

Mr. Humwhistel did not hear her. Dressed in his usual baggy trousers and a shabby summer jacket, he was busy leading a line of boys and girls from a point fairly high up on the slope to one closer to the river.

Professor Tuttle pulled nervously on his short mustache. "What on earth are they doing?" he asked.

"I started to tell you," Miss Pickerell said. "They go on rock-hunting expeditions. Not your kind of rocks, Professor Tuttle. Just rocks that are interesting because of their size or color or natural formation. My middle nephew, Euphus, has won three merit badges for finding some especially interesting ones."

Professor Tuttle hurried out of the car. "Mr. Humwhistel! Mr. Humwhistel!" he called, as he climbed down the slope side.

Miss Pickerell, taking her big black umbrella out of the rear of the car for balance, scrambled after him as quickly as she could. When she caught up, Professor Tuttle was standing in the middle of a heap of broken pieces of glass and pottery of all imaginable colors. He uttered a long-drawn-out whistle when he stooped to pick up a jagged piece of cloudy purple glass.

"I think," he said slowly, as he turned the glass first one way and then another and scrutinized it inch by inch, "I think we have something more than a site for a Boy Scout rock-hunting expedition here."

CHAPTER THREE

Race Against the Bulldozer

Professor Tuttle nearly slipped three times as he ran down the slope, clutching the piece of purple glass in his left hand and waving at Mr. Humwhistel with his right. Miss Pickerell did her best to keep up with him.

"Mr. Humwhistel! Mr. Humwhistel!" the professor shouted.

"Yoo Hoo!" Miss Pickerell called.

"Has he gone stone-deaf?" Professor Tuttle asked, when they stopped for breath. "I'm screaming at the top of my lungs."

"He's paying attention to the children," Miss Pickerell explained. "He's teaching them about the rocks."

"Ah, yes, rocks!" Professor Tuttle said suddenly. "Are you sure mine is safe with Mr. Rugby?"

"Perfectly safe, Professor," Miss Pickerell said. "Mr. Rugby promised to lock it in his storeroom. I heard him."

30

"Yes," Professor Tuttle remembered. "On the top shelf, between his very best recipes and his collection of moon pictures. I suppose it's all right."

He looked at his silver pocket watch. "I must be careful of the time," he said. "I have that next train to make. It's most important that I get to the state capital as soon as I can."

"I see," said Miss Pickerell, who wasn't entirely sure that she did. She was just wondering whether it would be very impolite of her to ask the professor what he was going to do in the state capital when she observed a change in the scene below her. The children were scattering toward the river bank. And Mr. Humwhistel was sitting down on a tree stump and spreading out a brightly colored map to examine.

"He'll hear us now," she announced, as she ran toward Mr. Humwhistel, calling, "Yoo Hoo!"

Professor Tuttle followed, echoing her call.

Mr. Humwhistel stood up suddenly, knocking over the map he was studying. He stared at the excited professor who was approaching him and at Miss Pickerell who was signaling to him with her black umbrella. Then he pushed his gold-rimmed spectacles down on his nose, looked over them to make certain he was seeing right, and rushed forward eagerly to meet his visitors.

"Why, Professor E-b-e-n-e-z-e-r T-u-t-t-l-e!" he exclaimed. "What are you doing *here?* And how nice to see you, Miss Pickerell! How very, very nice!"

Professor Tuttle wasted no words. "I've been searching for you all morning, Humwhistel," he said. "Fortunately, I met your good friend, Miss Pickerell. She brought me here. On the way, I picked up this fascinating bit of glass."

Mr. Humwhistel leaned down to look more closely at the glass in Professor Tuttle's upturned palm. He was very quick in his examination. "We dig up dozens of these every day," he said, when he had straightened up again. "Under and around the rocks."

Professor Tuttle went red in the face.

"Are you feeling all right?" Miss Pickerell asked.

He did not answer her. "Who found this glass, Mr. Humwhistel?" he asked, speaking very slowly.

Mr. Humwhistel reflected for a moment. "Euphus, I believe," he said, finally, and added by way of explanation, "That's Miss Pickerell's middle nephew."

"Yes, yes, I know," Professor Tuttle replied. "The one who earns all the merit badges."

"Three badges," Miss Pickerell corrected him.

"He may get a fourth this summer," Mr. Humwhistel suggested.

"See here," Professor Tuttle broke in. "Let's get back to the subject. Do you realize that this piece of glass we have been discussing may well be a significant archeological discovery?"

Both Miss Pickerell and Mr. Humwhistel stared at him in wonder.

"Look for yourself, Miss Pickerell," Professor Tuttle offered. "Look near the edges here and tell me what you see."

He held the glass out in front of her. Miss Pickerell saw very clearly what he was referring to.

"Do you mean the bubbles?" she added.

"Exactly!" Professor Tuttle exclaimed, running his free hand through his hair in his excitement. "You have a good eye, Miss Pickerell. Defects like bubbles or blisters in glass are an almost certain sign that the glass was made at least one hundred years ago, before our modern methods perfected the art of glass-making."

Mr. Humwhistel leaned down again and

squinted at the object in Professor Tuttle's palm. "Good gracious!" he mumbled.

"Pooh!" Miss Pickerell declared. "Anybody can own a pitcher or a bottle or a candy bowl made of old glass. Why, somebody might have been walking along with it and just dropped it."

"But you forget," the professor interrupted with a note of triumph in his voice. "You forget what Mr. Humwhistel just told us. Your nephew, Euphus, dug up this piece of glass!"

"Well," Miss Pickerell said, still not convinced, "he may not have been digging very deep. It could have been dropped by somebody only a few weeks ago."

"True," Professor Tuttle said. "You have an inquiring mind as well as an expert eye, Miss Pickerell. We will have to ask Euphus how deeply he dug."

"I should think that would be most important," Miss Pickerell said.

"Of course, there are other ideas to consider," the professor added.

Miss Pickerell was becoming very impatient. The professor had an even more complicated way of explaining things than Mr. Humwhistel. And much as she admired her friend, Mr. Humwhistel, she couldn't say that she particularly

34

enjoyed listening when he explained something.

"What other ideas, Professor?" she asked.

Professor Tuttle came to the point with surprising speed. "Idea, number one," he said, "or maybe, I should more appropriately call it clue, number one: I notice the ground has been cleared and trees cut down in this area. As a matter of fact, when we first caught up with Mr. Humwhistel, he was sitting on a tree stump. Soil-disturbing activity frequently unearths buried objects."

"Professor Tuttle," Mr. Humwhistel said "if I may interrupt, I think I should tell . . ."

"Not now," Professor Tuttle replied. "As I was saying, clue, number two: our friend, Mr. Rugby, told me when I was busy enjoying his thoroughly delicious Eclipse Specials, that it rained in this vicinity all through the month of June. Heavy rainfall, by loosening so much of the topsoil, can also serve to unearth . . ."

"Professor Tuttle," Mr. Humwhistel said again, "I really must tell . . ."

"Later," the professor insisted. "I have a train to make. I want to give you this information quickly so that your Scouts can carry on from there. Now then, clue, number three, and this may be the most important point: the glass was found on a slope, in a river valley. What does history tell us about the places where people have settled in the past? The story is always the same. Generation after generation, the favorite spot has been in a fertile valley, near a fresh-water river."

Miss Pickerell looked admiringly at the professor. "Naturally," she said. "That's the most reasonable place."

"What's more," Professor Tuttle continued, "people often build their cities, even their houses, one on top of the other, in exactly the same spot. People frequently abandon a place where they have lived. They may go away because of a war or a fire or an earthquake or any number of other good reasons."

An idea was beginning to take shape in Miss Pickerell's head. "And when they go away," she said, "they leave behind the things that belonged to them. That's only natural, too."

"They may leave behind all sorts of things," Professor Tuttle said. "Sometimes, it's their pots and pans. Sometimes, it's tools or weapons or just the foundations of their burning buildings."

Miss Pickerell was thinking hard. "You said something about people building their cities,

36

one on top of the other, in exactly the same spot," she said.

"Oh, yes," the professor replied. "They do that all the time. People may abandon a place, as I explained, but then, years later, other people come along, looking for a good place to live. They choose the same spot and build their new cities right on top of what's left of the old ones. Most often, what's left of the old city is buried under the ground by the time the new people get there. They may not even know that they're building their city on top of an old one."

"And people sometimes do this over and over again," Miss Pickerell exclaimed, "through hundreds and hundreds of years!"

"Even thousands," the professor said.

The idea in Miss Pickerell's head was becoming clearer and clearer. "So that if we dig deep enough," she said, hardly able to control her excitement now, "we can find out things about the way people lived at many different times in our history. Things we may never have known!"

"Yes," the professor said. "We go down layer by layer. Every layer represents a different time, with its own clues and its own story to tell."

"A dig is like a layer cake!" Miss Pickerell announced. "The top layer is the one that is put on last."

"A most apt description, Miss Pickerell," Professor Tuttle went on. "Of course, we have to examine everything that we find in these layers most carefully."

"But first, we have to keep digging," Miss Pickerell said, "to see . . ."

"Miss Pickerell!" Mr. Humwhistel said agitatedly. "You really have to listen to me. You don't realize . . ."

"Sh!" Miss Pickerell told him. "What I was going to say is that we must dig first to see what we find and then check."

This time, it was the sound of heavy treads scrunching on the gravel of the road that interrupted Miss Pickerell. She and the professor looked up quickly. Mr. Humwhistel did not move. He simply stood still and groaned.

A bulldozer, its gears grinding, its steel shovel pushing aside everything in sight, was coming toward them. It had left the road and was slowly making its way down the slope.

"That's what I've been trying to tell you," Mr. Humwhistel said, sighing. "There's no point in your thinking about what archeological treasures we can dig up in this valley. We won't have a chance to dig for anything. The county is widening the road. As Professor Tuttle observed, trees have been cut and ground cleared in preparation. The bulldozer is finishing the job of leveling a good part of this hillside right now!"

CHAPTER FOUR

An Important Assignment

"Why, that's ridiculous," Miss Pickerell exclaimed. "They just can't destroy this site!"

Professor Tuttle said that he agreed. Mr. Humwhistel looked sad.

"We've got to think of something," Miss Pickerell went on.

"What?" Mr. Humwhistel and Professor Tuttle asked together.

"I'm not sure," Miss Pickerell said. "But it seems to me the first thing we have to do is to get more specific information." She brushed some dust off her dress with a fresh, white handkerchief that she took out of her knitting bag, and resolutely began to climb the hill. She did not pause until she was at the very top.

At the right, on the opposite side of the road, stood her car and her trailer with the animals. Miss Pickerell went to them first. She patted each one affectionately. "I'll be taking you home for lunch very soon," she told them reassuringly. "Don't you worry!"

The cow looked trustfully into Miss Pickerell's face and mooed. Pumpkins rubbed his head against her shoulder and made friendly little cat sounds.

"Very, very soon," Miss Pickerell repeated. She waited quietly for a moment, thinking. Then she crossed the road and walked to the left where the bulldozer was still clattering away. At first, the driver did not hear her when she called to him.

"Excuse me for interrupting," she said in a loud voice when she had his attention, "but can you tell me exactly how much of this slope you are planning to use for your new road? It's very important that I know."

The driver pointed to a spot just past the place where Professor Tuttle had found the glass.

"Thank you," Miss Pickerell said, as she sighed hopelessly. Then suddenly, she thought of another question. "Will you tell me one thing more?" she asked. "Approximately when do you think you will be reaching that spot?"

"Not till Monday," the driver said. "We go off the job at four today. And, of course, we don't work on Saturday and Sunday."

"No, of course not," Miss Pickerell replied. "Thank you again."

She was feeling much more encouraged. A thousand thoughts raced through her head. She tried to sort them out as she hurried down the hill.

"I have a plan," she told Mr. Humwhistel and Professor Tuttle the moment she reached them. "What time is it, Professor?"

Both Mr. Humwhistel and Professor Tuttle examined their watches.

"It's 11:58 exactly," Professor Tuttle said.

Mr. Humwhistel coordinated his watch with the professor's. Miss Pickerell counted out loud

while she made rapid calculations on her fingers.

"We have sixty-seven hours," she announced. "If we start digging right now and keep going until seven o'clock Monday morning, we have sixty-seven hours."

"I'm afraid I don't understand," Mr. Humwhistel said.

"The bulldozer won't reach the place we're interested in until Monday," Miss Pickerell explained. "If we can get the Scouts to dig, they can start now and continue through the weekend."

Mr. Humwhistel counted much more rapidly than Miss Pickerell. "The sixty-seven hours between now and Monday," he said almost immediately, "include both days and nights. The children can dig, but not at . . ."

"No, no," Miss Pickerell said. *"We'll* work at night. You and I and maybe Mr. Rugby. We'll need floodlights to work in the dark, but I think I can take care of that."

Mr. Humwhistel still looked doubtful. "I don't know how much we can accomplish in sixty-seven hours," he said.

"That depends," Professor Tuttle said a bit more optimistically. "How many Scouts have you got here?"

"Twenty," Mr. Humwhistel replied. "Fifteen boys and five girls."

"All right," the professor said. "Let's get going. Give me that map of yours, will you, Humwhistel?"

Mr. Humwhistel handed his map over. Professor Tuttle turned it wrong side up and folded it several times to make a pad. Then he began to draw on the blank part that was on top.

"Here," he said, making a big, heavy dot in the center with his ball-point pen. "Here is the place where Euphus dug up the piece of glass. I

44

want four of your best Scouts to dig in that spot."

Mr. Humwhistel took his black memorandum book with its attached gold pencil out of his jacket pocket. He began thoughtfully to jot down names.

"Now, watch carefully," the professor continued, as he drew one long line from left to right through his center dot and another long line, crossing the center dot from top to bottom. At the end of each line, he made a small star.

"Is that the digging plan?" Miss Pickerell asked.

"Yes," the professor said. "The places I have marked with a star are four more digging sites. They should be approximately fifty paces apart."

"The Scouts count paces by their footsteps," Mr. Humwhistel remarked.

"Good enough," the professor said. "Now then, I want a team of four Scouts at each of these sites. They will be digging *in* toward the central spot. The master team, in the center, will be digging *out* toward them. Eventually, they should meet."

Mr. Humwhistel continued to make notes.

"What about tools, Professor?" Miss Pickerell asked briskly.

"Ah, yes—tools," Professor Tuttle replied. "Shovels, hoes, picks, painting trowels, knives, brushes, and sieves. The sieves are for examining the soil closely for finds that may be very small. The brushes are for gently clearing off the dirt from fragile or breakable objects. The knives and trowels are for scraping. Picks are for . . ."

"We have picks," Mr. Humwhistel said.

"I have an idea where we can get some of the rest of the tools," Miss Pickerell said.

She borrowed Professor Tuttle's pen and asked Mr. Humwhistel to tear out a page from his memo book for her. She leaned the page against the folded map and wrote neatly, "ASSIGNMENTS. No. 1: Tools."

"Write these down, too, Miss Pickerell," directed Professor Tuttle, looking over her shoulder. "No. 2: Photography. No. 3: Record-keeping."

Miss Pickerell wrote while the professor went on to explain what he meant.

"We photograph everything we find," he said. "We also keep a separate record for each object that we unearth. In the record, we include the photograph and/or a drawing of the object. We note when it was found, its color, shape, and texture, the place where it was discovered, and the exact position in which it was discovered."

"Suppose we assign one person to do the photography or drawing," Miss Pickerell suggested, "and one person to keep the records. That way, we'll be sure of just who's responsible for what." She wrote, "RESPONSIBILITIES"—underlining it.

The professor looked at his watch. "Let's get your Scouts started with their picks," he said to Mr. Humwhistel.

"I'll drive back to Mr. Rugby's diner," Miss Pickerell declared. "I thought we might ask him if we could borrow his paring knives, pastry brushes, and flour sieves."

"A very good idea," Mr. Humwhistel said.

"Are you sure you'll remember your various assignments?" the professor asked. He began ticking them off on his fingers. "Tools, cameras, floodlights. Ah yes, a generator to which to attach the floodlights."

Miss Pickerell made a mental note about the generator.

"Charting paper for the records, rulers for . . . ," Professor Tuttle went on.

Miss Pickerell, already trudging up the hill, turned back to nod that she had heard.

47

It was not until she reached the road and started to rearrange her thoughts that Miss Pickerell realized all she had to do. Tools, generator, camera—she wasn't even sure where she ought to start. "I'll begin at the beginning," she said to herself. "Yes, I'll do just that and solve each problem as I get to it. I won't get upset in advance!"

CHAPTER FIVE

"Stop at Once!"

Miss Pickerell found Mr. Rugby seated behind his cash register, checking on his receipts. He sprang up the instant he saw her.

"Mr. Rugby," she said, deciding to tackle the problem of tools immediately. "Do you have five paring knives, five pastry brushes, and five flour sieves? I'd like to borrow them."

Mr. Rugby stared dumbfounded. "Did you say five paring knives, five pastry . . . ?" he repeated, when he found his voice again.

Miss Pickerell nodded.

"They're . . . they're in my cutlery closet," Mr. Rugby spluttered. "If you'll come with me, I'll . . ."

"It's only fair to tell you, Mr. Rugby," Miss Pickerell said, as she followed him into his spotless pantry and watched him count out the articles she wanted and place them for her in a big shopping bag. "It's only fair to tell you that, if you don't mind, we're going to use them as archeological tools. One set to a team. On a dig."

Mr. Rugby's eyes grew round with wonder. "A dig!" he breathed. "Who? Where?"

49

"All of us," Miss Pickerell said, wishing Mr. Rugby didn't always have to ask so many questions. "On the slope leading from the road to the river. Professor Tuttle and Mr. Humwhistel are there with the Scouts now."

"A dig!" Mr. Rugby exclaimed again. "Right in Square Toe County! Wait till the Governor hears about this! Maybe you ought to call him, Miss Pickerell."

Miss Pickerell sighed. Another thing she usually found herself wishing when she talked to Mr. Rugby was that he didn't get so excited quite so fast.

"I'll call the Governor when I have something to tell him, Mr. Rugby," she said. "I wouldn't dream of wasting his time, otherwise. At the moment, we have only a clue."

"This clue may be most important," insisted Mr. Rugby.

"Naturally," Miss Pickerell said. "Or we wouldn't be digging. Please excuse me, Mr. Rugby. I don't have much time. I still have all these other things to attend to."

Miss Pickerell showed him the page on which she had noted her assignments. Mr. Rugby became more excited than ever.

"I'm sure I can do something else for you, Miss Pickerell," he said, as he eagerly pointed to

50

item No. 1 on Miss Pickerell's list. "I know somebody who'll be happy to lend you trowels, shovels, hoes, a generator, and all the floodlights that you want. He has too many of them in stock, as it is. I imagine you are acquainted with my friend, Mr. Kettelson."

"The hardware-store man?" Miss Pickerell asked.

"One of my most satisfied customers," Mr. Rugby assured her. "And very grateful to me. I showed him a new game of solitaire to play when business is slow. It keeps him from worrying."

"Goodness!" Miss Pickerell said.

"I'll bring everything to the dig in my station wagon," Mr. Rugby offered. "It won't take more than a few minutes. My part-time assistant can take care of things while I'm gone."

"That's very kind of you," Miss Pickerell said, feeling considerably relieved. She crossed item No. 1 off her list and began to make her way out of the pantry. Mr. Rugby, holding the shopping bag, lagged behind.

"Miss Pickerell," he said, a little hesitantly. "I hope you won't mind if I ask you a question."

"If your question is about why we need floodlights and a generator when the sun is shining,

Mr. Rugby," Miss Pickerell answered, as she continued to hurry toward the door, "I can explain it very easily."

She told Mr. Rugby all about the race against the advancing bulldozer while he walked her back to the car. He volunteered his services as one of the night diggers immediately.

"I'll get Mr. Kettelson to come in and relieve me during the evening," he said. "He's an excellent cook. And I'll call Mr. Esticott, too. If the train mix-up ever gets straightened out, I'm sure he could spare some time from his baggage-master duties."

Miss Pickerell drove off to the accompaniment of Mr. Rugby's cheerful smiles and hand-waving. She felt very encouraged. Thinking ahead to the things she still had to do, she outlined them carefully in her mind. She was so busy concentrating, it seemed only a few minutes had passed when she reached the familiar bumps of the road leading up to Square Toe Farm.

The house was very quiet. Miss Pickerell felt tempted to go in and see what Rosemary was doing. But she took her cow down to the pasture first, and she grabbed a handful of cat niblets from a box that she kept in the barn and put them in a saucer for Pumpkins. Then she walked back to the house and up the wooden steps that led into the kitchen.

Rosemary was having lunch. When she heard about the dig, she wanted to go along. But Miss Pickerell asked her to stay at the farm and look after the animals. Rosemary promised faithfully to milk the cow and give Pumpkins his dinner.

"You can borrow my camera with the detachable flash bulbs, if you like," Rosemary offered. "The one that saved your life on the far side of the moon. And be sure to wear an apron to keep your dress clean during the digging."

"You're absolutely right," said Miss Pickerell, and she put Rosemary's camera in her knitting bag, quickly donned her apron, and headed for the door. "I'll telephone whenever I can, from Mr. Rugby's diner."

"Fine," said Rosemary, waving good-by.

Miss Pickerell ran out the door and down toward the barn for her car.

All the way to Square Toe River, Miss Pickerell tried to think of ways to speed up the night shift. Every once in a while, an idea came into her head. It seemed to pop out almost as fast, though.

"Maybe it will come back to me when I talk things over with the professor," she told herself consolingly, as she parked the car at the top of the slope and began to walk down to the dig.

But the professor was in no mood to discuss anything when she got there. He was standing on the exact spot where Euphus had found the piece of purple glass, looking very angry. On his right, stood Mr. Humwhistel and a group of Scouts, all with their heads down. On his left, Mr. Rugby was fussing with at least twenty-five floodlights which blinked on and off at dizzying speed. Each time they went on, Mr. Rugby said happily, "Now they'll stay lit!" But they didn't.

The professor appealed to Miss Pickerell the moment he noticed her. "Tell me, please," he pleaded, "do you know any way of persuading your friend, Mr. Rugby, that he is not as much of an expert in the connecting of generators as he is in the preparation of Eclipse Specials? And have you any idea as to how I can impress upon the Scouts the importance of record-keeping? Just take a look at this, will you, Miss Pickerell?"

The professor pointed to a small heap of broken objects at Mr. Humwhistel's feet.

"Finds?" Miss Pickerell gasped.

"Yes," the professor said. "One bronze door knocker, the handle and spout of what may once have been an interestingly shaped teapot, a set of

54

ornamented bronze keys, a handful of rather oddly colored children's marbles, a . . ."

The professor paused in his listing. He glared at the Scouts' bowed heads.

"Only," he went on, his voice nearly exploding with anger, "only we've no idea just how any of these things looked or even where they came from before they were piled up in this spot. We don't know which objects were found near the surface, which objects were discovered a little farther down, and which were unearthed at still deeper layers. How can we even begin to determine how old they are if we don't keep track of the layers?"

"We'll just have to start all over again, Professor," Miss Pickerell said, sounding determined.

"Start what all over again?" a voice coming down the slope asked loudly. "Whatever you're doing, stop it at once!"

Miss Pickerell looked up to see the sheriff approaching.

"Good afternoon, Sheriff," she said, smiling.

"Good afternoon, Miss Pickerell," he answered politely. "Tell me, who's in charge here?"

Miss Pickerell looked from Professor Tuttle to Mr. Humwhistel to Mr. Rugby. Each of them looked questioningly back at her.

"Whatever you're doing, stop it at once!"

"I suppose I am, Sheriff," she said. "At least, I think so."

"Do you have a permit for digging?" the sheriff asked.

"Why, no," Miss Pickerell said, "I had no idea . . ."

The sheriff took a handbook of regulations out of his hip pocket. He wet his thumb and leafed through the book until he came to the page he wanted. "Right here, Miss Pickerell," he said. "Article No. 16, Section No. 3, Public Law No. 2376A states that no digging or excavation of any kind may take place on county property without an official permit issued by the Department of Public Works. Any and all violators are subject to arrest."

"Arrest?" Miss Pickerell repeated, shaking her head in disbelief.

"That's right," the sheriff replied. "And where the law is concerned, ignorance is no excuse."

"I agree completely, Sheriff," Miss Pickerell said firmly.

The sheriff relaxed a little. "I won't arrest you this time, Miss Pickerell," he said. "But you can't go on digging without a permit. You'll have to stop. As of this exact minute!"

CHAPTER SIX

The Governor Helps

For several minutes after the sheriff left, nobody said a word. Miss Pickerell moved over to the stump of a tree and sat down. Professor Tuttle walked round and round the four corner digging places, looking lost in thought. Mr. Humwhistel lit his pipe. The Scouts shuffled their feet. Mr. Rugby, opening and closing his mouth a number of times without speaking, finally broke the silence.

"What are we to do?" he asked.

"I know what we *must* do," Miss Pickerell said, sitting bolt upright and taking a firm grip on the handle of her umbrella. "We must get a digging permit."

The scouts applauded. Mr. Humwhistel stared at them with an expression of sudden attentiveness. "I'd forgotten about you children," he said. "It's time you went home."

The Scouts protested.

"Your mothers will be worrying about you," Miss Pickerell told them, while she decisively waved some of the reluctant members up the slope.

58

"Well," Professor Tuttle said when the last Scout had climbed out of sight, "I suppose I ought to be picking up my rock and . . ."

"You can't leave now," Miss Pickerell told him. "Not when we're in trouble."

The professor looked embarrassed. "But it's after four o'clock," he sighed. "It's probably much too late to apply for a permit. And it's certainly too late to get it in time to enable us to do much digging. The investigation that precedes the granting of a permit usually takes days."

"This permit is different," Miss Pickerell said. "We have a time limit. We can explain that to the Commissioner of Public Works."

"I happen to know," Mr. Rugby said, "that the Commissioner didn't go to his office today. He told me at breakfast that he was on his way to Appleyard State Park. He had to supervise the arrangements there for the State Troopers' annual cook-out. He left his clerk in the office to deal with any emergencies."

"I hardly think the clerk is going to consider a request for a digging permit made at 4:15 on a Friday afternoon an emergency," Professor Tuttle said gloomily. "Do you have any other ideas, Miss Pickerell?"

Mr. Rugby, looking at Miss Pickerell and talking to Professor Tuttle, said, "I think she should . . ."

Miss Pickerell said, "I *know* what you're thinking, Mr. Rugby. Kindly let me make up my own mind."

Mr. Rugby said, "I didn't mean . . ."

Miss Pickerell said, "I know you didn't. I'm sorry."

She did not like to admit it, but Mr. Rugby was probably right. There was no other way. She would have to call the Governor. She would call him at home. It was easier to talk to him there. If he wasn't home, she'd try his office.

"All right," she announced to Mr. Rugby, Mr. Humwhistel, and Professor Tuttle. "I'll discuss our problem with the Governor."

"We can all discuss it with him," Mr. Rugby said. "I have five telephone extensions in the diner—one at the dining-room desk, one in the kitchen, one in the pantry, one . . ."

"Come on," Professor Tuttle said, leading the way up to the cars at the top of the hill. "Let's get going!"

Miss Pickerell's hand was a bit uncertain when she tried to dial the Governor's number back at the diner. She hadn't had a chance to summarize her thoughts so that she could ex-

plain things to the Governor without taking up too much of his time. Also, she felt very uncomfortable making this call in Mr. Rugby's pantry while Professor Tuttle sat at another extension in the kitchen and Mr. Rugby and Mr. Humwhistel paced back and forth between the two rooms.

The Governor answered the phone promptly. "Governor's residence," he stated. "Governor speaking."

"Good afternoon, Governor," Miss Pickerell said, her voice coming out of her throat much higher than she expected. She tried her best to push it down.

"This is Miss Pickerell," she added, speaking in her more usual tones.

"Why hello, Miss Pickerell," the Governor said warmly. "What can I do for you on this bright, cheery afternoon?"

"We need a digging permit, Governor," Miss Pickerell said directly.

"A digging permit?" the Governor repeated. "Did you say a digging . . . ?"

"Yes, Governor," Professor Tuttle broke in, introducing himself and describing the emergency clearly and precisely.

"Well, well," the Governor said. "What an interesting idea! My dear Miss Pickerell, what will you think of next?"

"It isn't really my idea," Miss Pickerell told him quickly. "I'm just helping."

"We all know what your help can mean, Miss Pickerell," the Governor replied. "And now it's up to me, I suppose. About the digging permit, that is. Of course, it's rather late in the day."

"That's just the point, Governor," Miss Pickerell interrupted. "We have only until Monday morning. I didn't like to bother you, but this *is* an emergency."

"Yes, yes, I understand," the Governor said. "Well, I imagine I can get word to the sheriff. I can tell him that a permit will be applied for and granted through the regular channels and that you may dig in the meantime. Will that be all right, Miss Pickerell?"

"That will be perfect," Miss Pickerell said happily. "Thank you very much, Governor."

Miss Pickerell hung up. Professor Tuttle, in the kitchen, did the same. Mr. Rugby, who had been listening in to the last part of the conversation on his desk telephone, called out for everybody to join him.

"If I might make a suggestion," he said, "it seems to me that everybody would be better off right now with a bite to eat."

Miss Pickerell admitted that she had had no lunch. Professor Tuttle said that the excitement had made him hungry. Mr. Humwhistel thought an early dinner might well be something to consider. Mr. Rugby added that an early dinner was exactly what he had been planning.

"Everything is ready," Mr. Rugby said. "My assistant can serve you." He ushered them into a booth and excused himself. "I'd like to get back to the site immediately," he explained. "I have an idea about how to position the floodlights. It came to me while I was listening to the Governor."

Miss Pickerell agreed that the best ideas often came accidentally, and wished Mr. Rugby luck. Professor Tuttle said some of his very good ideas came to him after he had pushed a problem into the back of his mind. He, Miss Pickerell, and Mr. Humwhistel talked about this all through dinner.

CHAPTER SEVEN

Curious Objects

The minute Miss Pickerell, Mr. Humwhistel, and Professor Tuttle began to walk down the hill, they saw Mr. Rugby's floodlights. The sun was still shining, but Mr. Rugby had the lights on full force.

After they had all congratulated Mr. Rugby on his success, Professor Tuttle suggested a brief conference.

"I'll tell you my plan," he said to them all. "The best thing we can do at this point is to dig a test pit. That will give us some quick information."

"Anything to save time," Mr. Rugby agreed immediately.

Miss Pickerell thought Mr. Rugby was too hasty in accepting an idea he didn't know anything about. "Just what is a test pit?" she asked.

"I'll show you," Professor Tuttle said, taking out his pen and borrowing a large piece of cross-lined paper from Mr. Humwhistel. He leaned the paper against a nearby rock and began to

draw a diagram. Miss Pickerell, Mr. Humwhistel, and Mr. Rugby watched carefully.

"This is the slope," the professor went on as he drew a long curved line. "The place I have marked with a circle is the site where we are now digging. We are going to discontinue that now. We are going to dig on the side of the slope instead. Right along this dark line I have made."

He handed the diagram over to Miss Pickerell who studied it and gave it to Mr. Humwhistel. Mr. Humwhistel looked at it carefully and passed it on to Mr. Rugby. Mr. Rugby said he didn't understand it all. Mr. Humwhistel said, "Hmmm." Miss Pickerell waited for the professor to continue.

"We'll dig a test pit about three feet wide, and shore it up with boards as we go," Professor Tuttle explained. "By working in concentrated fashion on such a small area, we'll be able

to dig quite far down and explore different layers of soil. The things we dig up at the different
layers will be indications to us of what we may
discover when we dig on the larger site later."

Mr. Humwhistel said, "Hmmm" again.

"How far apart will the layers be?" asked
Miss Pickerell.

"Anywhere from a few inches up to many,
many feet," Professor Tuttle said. "It all depends on the people who inhabited the place at
the time."

"Whether they were city people or village
people?" Mr. Humwhistel asked. "Is that it?"

"Yes," the professor said. "City people usually had organized systems for disposing of
things they wanted to throw away. In small
villages, the carpenter or the shoemaker or the
blacksmith may have allowed scrap wood or
leather or metal to accumulate in waste heaps.
Practices of this kind over a period of years
tended to leave behind much thicker layers."

"I should think natural conditions would
affect the depth of a layer, too," Miss Pickerell
said. "From my reading on geology, I seem to
remember hearing that a flood or a fire can easily
reduce the size of a soil layer."

"Right!" Professor Tuttle said. "You certainly are up on things, Miss Pickerell. Floods

can wash the soil away and fires can burn up the topsoil of a particular layer. What is even more important, natural conditions can change the color of the soil. And we find different colors as we keep on digging. Each color is a separate layer."

"The top layer is fresh dirt, of course," Miss Pickerell said, thinking about her farm.

"Of course," the professor agreed. "Its exact color depends on how rich the soil is in a particular part of the country. But any light soil we may find underneath is usually wind-blown sand or dust. And dark layers below that can mean ashes resulting from destruction by fire. We find a lot of that dark soil when we are digging in levels that existed during periods of war."

"I suppose we unearth most of the finds in the dark layers," Miss Pickerell suggested.

"Not necessarily," Professor Tuttle said, shaking his head and walking over to the pile of unrecorded objects that the Scouts had dug up. "I have an idea that most of this lot was found fairly near the top."

He paused to examine the marbles more closely. "These may have come from farther down," he said half to himself. "They seem to suggest the same period as Euphus' piece of glass."

He kept on looking at the marbles and muttered to himself for several minutes.

"Professor Tuttle," Miss Pickerell broke in a little irritably, "don't you think we'd better start digging again?"

"Ah, yes! You're right," Professor Tuttle exclaimed. He gave Mr. Rugby and Mr. Humwhistel each a set of tools and told them to start digging. He also selected a set of tools for himself.

Miss Pickerell settled herself on a low, flat rock nearby, with her camera, a thick pad of charting paper, and a number of freshly sharpened pencils at her side. She wanted to dig, too, but Professor Tuttle felt she would be more useful as the official record keeper and photographer.

Miss Pickerell watched the diggers closely. She did not want to miss anything they might pick up. They worked very hard, gathering up shovelful after shovelful of soil and carefully sifting them through their sieves. But not even the smallest find appeared.

Waiting was tedious. Miss Pickerell tried to think of something to do to pass the time. She decided to imagine the rock garden she was hoping to plant next spring. It would have jonquils and red primroses and little golden rock roses with splashes of pink on the edge of their petals. Her thoughts were very far away when she heard the sound of approaching footsteps.

It was Mr. Esticott. He wore his baggage master's cap with the golden braid on its navy blue brim and an old double-breasted uniform jacket which did not quite meet across his stomach. "Good evening, Miss Pickerell," he said. "I hope I didn't startle you."

"Not at all, Mr. Esticott," Miss Pickerell said emphatically.

"I trust your animals are well," Mr. Esticott went on, and cleared his throat in his usual way.

"Pumpkins and the cow are very well," Miss Pickerell began to tell him.

"Miss Pickerell! Miss Pickerell!" the professor's voice boomed from inside the test pit. "Over here! I need you."

"Coming!" Miss Pickerell answered.

"Bring the camera," the professor boomed again.

Miss Pickerell stopped to pick up the camera. She scrambled over two neatly stacked-up piles of earth that Professor Tuttle had removed from the test pit and hastened to his side. Mr. Esticott followed.

"Take a close up photograph of this object, Miss Pickerell," the professor said as soon as he saw her. "I'll get out of your way."

"A find!" Miss Pickerell said joyfully, as she adjusted the lens to the proper opening. She squinted through the view finder and clicked the button smartly.

"Good!" Professor Tuttle said. "Now we have a picture of the object in the place where it was found. We must always take the first photograph that way. The place where an object is found can be an important clue to other objects we may unearth in the same vicinity."

"I understand," said Miss Pickerell, making a mental note to herself to think it out more clearly later. "Professor Tuttle, I don't believe you've met Mr. Esticott. He's here to help us dig."

"Glad to know you," Professor Tuttle said, and went on with what he was saying without looking up. "We'll label this photograph, the object itself, and the chart which you will prepare as a permanent record, all with the code ST-I. ST will stand for Square Toe Excavation Site."

"That's very logical," Miss Pickerell said approvingly.

At that instant, both Mr. Rugby and Mr. Humwhistel shouted out, one after the other.

"Look what I found!" said Mr. Rugby.

"See here!" said Mr. Humwhistel.

"Don't touch!" called the professor. "Pictures first!"

Miss Pickerell snapped two rapid pictures of the separate finds made by Mr. Rugby and Mr. Humwhistel. Mr. Esticott looked on.

Professor Tuttle walked over to Mr. Rugby's find and bent down until his nose was less than an inch away from it. Then he followed the same procedure while he examined Mr. Humwhistel's discovery. At last he straightened up, dusted off his hands, and smiled at Miss Pickerell.

"Well, we have made a beginning," he said. "It's only a bone toothpick, a gold snuffbox, and a rusty metal hinge, but it could give us a glimpse into the lives of the people of Square Toe County, perhaps a hundred years ago. That's not such a bad start for the first day of a dig is it?"

"No," Miss Pickerell said quietly, as she thought about the people who once must have used the decorated snuffbox and the old bone toothpick. In the very next breath, she asked a question that suddenly popped into her head. "Don't we have to *prove* the age of these objects, Professor?"

Mr. Rugby, looking up from his place in the pit, applauded.

Mr. Humwhistel said, "Observation is important. But observation alone can lead us astray." Professor Tuttle said nothing.

CHAPTER EIGHT

Record-Keeping and Rain

Miss Pickerell was puzzled. "What did you have in mind for proving our theories, Professor?" she asked.

Professor Tuttle still did not answer. He looked up at the sky where the first star was now shining steadily and buttoned his jacket as a protection against the chill night air. Miss Pickerell watched him impatiently. Mr. Esticott cleared his throat again and coughed loudly.

The professor came to with a start. "I was just trying to remember a name," he said apologetically. He turned to Mr. Humwhistel. "You know the man I mean, Humwhistel," he said. "You brought him with you to the last meeting of the National Committee for the Advancement of Scientific Frontiers. The one who kept borrowing pipe tobacco from you, and pencils, which he never returned, from me. Then he said he couldn't read his notes and wanted to see mine."

"Mr. J. Adam Butterworth," Mr. Humwhistel exclaimed, "author of *Facts about Artifacts*

75

and owner of the largest known collection of photographs and documents on the artifacts of the last five hundred years."

"Artifacts?" Mr. Esticott repeated, looking questioningly at Miss Pickerell and the professor.

"That's what archeologists call man-made objects," Professor Tuttle explained hastily. "But coming back to J. Adam Butterworth, Humwhistel, where can we find him?"

"On Friday nights, at the meeting of the Antiquarian Research Society in Square Toe City," Mr. Humwhistel answered. "He's vice-president."

"Good!" Professor Tuttle said. "As soon as we have properly labeled and charted the objects, you can take them to him. He'll know soon enough whether my hunch about them is correct."

"Hunch?" Mr. Esticott asked.

"My dear sir," Professor Tuttle replied crossly. "Of course, my opinion about these artifacts is a hunch. It is speculation based on my observation of their material and workmanship. The design of this rusty metal hinge, for example, would lead me to believe that it was made in the eighteenth century. All science starts with this kind of educated hunch."

76

"But all hunches must be verified, Mr. Esticott," Miss Pickerell insisted.

"Exactly," Professor Tuttle said. "Mr. J. Adam Butterworth is the man who can compare our finds with artifacts of already known dates. He will see which period they fit into and should be able to tell us how old our artifacts are."

Miss Pickerell did not feel too pleased with this explanation.

"It seems to me, Professor," she said, "that there ought to be more scientific methods of dating archeological finds. Why, I read in one of your very own Sunday magazine articles that you sent an object to a laboratory to be dated under a microscope."

"That was an object made of obsidian, Miss Pickerell," the professor explained. "Obsidian is volcanic glass, and volcanic glass absorbs moisture which forms a layer at the edges. We can see this moisture or hydration layer under the microscope. The thicker the layer, the older the object."

"Couldn't we authenticate Euphus' piece of purple glass that way?" Miss Pickerell wanted to know.

"We could," Professor Tuttle said. "The laboratory would slice off a sample thin enough to put between the glass slides of the microscope and then examine it. But . . ." The professor looked doubtful.

"But you don't think the layers are very thick," Miss Pickerell added.

"Not unless this piece of glass is really ancient," Professor Tuttle said. "And the place where we found it doesn't make that very likely. Well, we have to get on!"

Professor Tuttle carefully lifted up the snuffbox, the hinge, and the toothpick and dusted each, in turn, with gentle strokes of his pastry brush.

"Prepare labels for these, will you, Humwhistel?" he called out. "Mark them ST-No. 1, ST-No. 2, and ST-No. 3. We'll send Euphus' piece of glass along, too. Mark that ST-No. 4. Date the labels and tie the labels onto the objects with some string. Now then, let's get to the charting. Are you ready, Miss Pickerell?"

Miss Pickerel reached for her pen and pad of charting paper. "Ready, Professor," she said, as she quickly straightened her glasses.

"We'll start with the snuffbox," the professor stated. "Mark your paper: FIELD SLIP, Square Toe River Valley Excavation, Pit A. Write ST-No. 1 in the upper left-hand corner and today's date in the upper right-hand corner. All right?"

"Done," Miss Pickerell said, finishing the writing of the date and looking up at the professor for further instructions.

"Next," the professor said. "Make a capital letter A. Put a colon after it and print the word OBJECT. What will you write next to it, Miss Pickerell?"

"One gold snuffbox," Miss Pickerell replied immediately.

"That's it," the professor said. "Now, capital letter B and the word LOCATION. Write: Pit A, three feet down from top."

The professor stopped dictating to talk to Mr. Rugby and Mr. Humwhistel who were watching Miss Pickerell write and making suggestions to her about the proper punctuation.

"Kindly get on with your digging and labeling, gentlemen," he said. "Every minute is important."

"Capital letter C," he said to Miss Pickerell, "then the word DESCRIPTION. Let's say it's a gold snuffbox with dimensions of . . . Hold it a second, Miss Pickerell."

Professor Tuttle took a flexible metal ruler out of his pocket, snapped it open, and proceeded to measure the find. "Describe it as two inches wide," he said to Miss Pickerell. "Leave a four-by-four-inch space on the bottom of the

Professor Tuttle proceeded to measure the find

page, right-hand side, for the photograph—also marked ST-No.1—which you will attach as soon as it is developed. In the meantime, please draw a sketch of the object on the left side of the paper. Have I forgotten anything?"

Miss Pickerell noticed two dents on the lid of the box. "Shouldn't we mention these?" she asked, pointing to them.

"Definitely," the professor said. "Most definitely. And the traces of floral decoration, as well. Note them under OTHER DETAILS. Now, Miss Pickerell, do you think you can go on alone from here? To chart the other objects in the same way?"

Miss Pickerell felt indignant enough to want to ask the professor what he meant. Why, any school child could go on independently with this clearly enumerated record-keeping! She decided to postpone her discussion about his attitudes, however, to a time when they were not so rushed. "I shall certainly do my best, Professor," she said.

Then she looked up in surprise. "Why, it's raining," she exclaimed.

"The sky was full of stars only a second ago," the professor complained.

"That's not unusual in the summer," Miss

Pickerell said. "But what a pity, just when we were beginning to get somewhere."

Mr. Rugby, Mr. Humwhistel, and Mr. Esticott bustled around gathering up tools and charts.

"This is the kind of rain that's likely to last for hours," Mr. Esticott stated. "We'll have to go home."

"I'm going back for a tarpaulin," Mr. Rugby announced. "To cover the trench and the tools. Mr. Kettelson's sure to have one in his shop."

"Better get into your car, Miss Pickerell," Mr. Humwhistel suggested. "You'll catch a cold."

"More hours lost," Professor Tuttle grumbled, as he helped Miss Pickerell up the rest of the slope. "We'll have to give up the idea of digging in a larger area altogether. We'll continue in the test pit. That's all we'll have time for."

Mr. Esticott got into the truck with Mr. Rugby. Professor Tuttle and Mr. Humwhistel joined Miss Pickerell in her car. Miss Pickerell noticed that Mr. Rugby had a basket stuffed with newspapers over his arm.

"The finds," he told her. "I've wrapped them very carefully."

"What about the records?" the professor asked.

82

"I have those, too," Mr. Humwhistel said. "If you'll drop me at my office where I can pick up my motorcycle, I'll hurry on to the Antiquarian Society. I don't want to miss Mr. Butterworth."

"I'll go with you," Professor Tuttle said. "I want to show him my rock."

Miss Pickerell turned on the headlights of her car. "Oh!" she said in a half-choked voice.

"Oh!" Mr. Humwhistel and Professor Tuttle said with her.

Planted almost directly in front of them and looking, in the beam of the headlights, even bigger and more menacing than in daylight, stood the bulldozer.

"Oh, you . . . you . . . ," Miss Pickerell spluttered angrily.

"We'll get a lot more interesting digging done before that's ready to move again," Mr. Humwhistel said comfortingly.

"Maybe," Professor Tuttle said.

Miss Pickerell continued to stare at the bulldozer. "You, you . . . bully!" she said contemptuously, finding the word she was looking for at precisely the same instant she turned on the ignition and began steering the car back to the road.

CHAPTER NINE

Down to the Indians

The telephone rang the next morning while Miss Pickerell was giving Pumpkins his breakfast. He stopped sniffing at the food he was about to eat and backed away from his plate. Miss Pickerell stooped down to pat him.

"I'll answer it," Rosemary said from where she was standing near the sink. "Why don't you stay with that cat and see that he eats? I didn't want to tell you yesterday, but he wouldn't eat a thing while you were gone. He wants to be fussed over."

The call turned out to be for Miss Pickerell. Pumpkins jumped up on the window sill and viewed both Miss Pickerell and the telephone with a cold eye when she left him to go and say, "Hello."

"Hello," Mr. Humwhistel's quiet voice answered. "I hope I'm not calling you too early."

"Oh, no, Mr. Humwhistel," Miss Pickerell said.

"How are the animals?" Mr. Humwhistel asked.

"Fine, thank you," Miss Pickerell said, trying

84

not to let her impatience show in her voice. Mr. Humwhistel loved animals, she knew, but she was sure he wasn't calling her up this Saturday morning just to find out how Pumpkins and the cow were feeling.

"That's good," Mr. Humwhistel said, like Mr. Esticott clearing his throat.

Miss Pickerell waited.

"I'm calling about two things," Mr. Humwhistel said finally. "The first is Mr. Butterworth's opinion of the finds. I thought you'd like to know."

"Yes?" Miss Pickerell asked. "Yes?"

"He feels sure the snuffbox, the toothpick, and the hinge are from the eighteenth century —they belonged to people who lived in Square Toe County then. It looks as if we've stumbled on some local buried treasure," Mr. Humwhistel went on.

"And to think how many times I passed by that spot," Miss Pickerell exclaimed excitedly. "Perhaps if we go on digging, we may find some Indian artifacts!"

"We may even be able to learn about the people who lived here before our history-book stories begin," Mr. Humwhistel added. "But the second thing I'm calling about, Miss Pickerell, is something that has just come up at the site.

Professor Tuttle is very disturbed. We're experiencing some interference with the dig."

"Not the bulldozer!" Miss Pickerell said quickly. "That's not supposed to be in operation today."

"Not the bulldozer," Mr. Humwhistel assured her. "No, what I'm talking about is a traffic snarl. All the Saturday drivers are stopping by to look at the diggers. And the Scouts all seem to have brought their parents to watch them dig. The sheriff is furious—both about the traffic and the danger to the diggers. So many spectators are crowding the edge of the pit . . ."

"I'll be there right away," Miss Pickerell said immediately, hanging up the receiver.

She stopped only to talk to Pumpkins, who purred when she fed him, and then proceeded to wash his whiskers. She said good-by to her cow when she walked down to the barn to get the car.

Miss Pickerell knew what Mr. Humwhistel meant about the traffic problem the moment she reached the fork in the road where Mr. Rugby's sign about the free cup of coffee appeared. Cars were moving bumper to bumper there. Near the intersection that led down from the bridge to the river, they had stopped moving altogether.

Leaning out of her window, Miss Pickerell could see the sheriff standing at the intersection frantically waving people on foot back into their cars. The spectators took their time about moving on, though. Each driver stopped for a last, lingering look at the diggers before starting up his automobile.

"This will never do!" Miss Pickerell exclaimed.

She searched in her knitting bag and found the whistle that she sometimes used to call Pumpkins in from wherever he was playing outdoors. It had a sharp, piercing tone.

"I can only hope it won't fetch all the cats in the neighborhood," she said to herself, as she walked out of the car, stationed herself past the sheriff at the top of the hill, and blew.

Everybody, including the sheriff, turned around immediately.

Miss Pickerell waved her arms.

Everybody stared. Then they laughed. But one by one, motorists quietly began to get into their cars. Miss Pickerell waved for them to move on.

"Quickly!" she called, as she blew her whistle again.

Pedestrians moved back. Cars moved forward. The sheriff waved on the cars behind them. Miss Pickerell hastened back into her own car, drove to the top of the slope, and ran down to the site as rapidly as she could.

She saw Mr. Humwhistel first. He was directing three teams of workers. The first consisted of Mr. Rugby, Mr. Esticott, and the bigger Boy Scouts. They were busy digging. The second team, made up of all the smaller boys, was removing the earth from the finds. The third team was all girls. They were sifting the earth to make sure the second team had not missed anything.

"We're up to the Indians," Mr. Rugby said, emerging from the pit to announce the news.

"Down to the Indians, you mean," argued Mr. Esticott, who followed.

"Has anyone shown Miss Pickerell our discoveries?" Professor Tuttle asked.

"Euphus is standing guard over them," Mr. Humwhistel said. "He's been our official record keeper this morning."

Euphus showed Miss Pickerell some cups of buffalo horn, several copper bowls, ladles, and spoons, two cradle boards, a pile of arrowheads, another pile of blunt-tipped arrows, and what looked like a doll. Professor Tuttle blew some of the dirt off the doll by puffing on it softly, and

showed Miss Pickerell that it had movable arms and legs.

"And these blunt-tipped arrows," he said, "were also toys. The Indian boys played with them. The blunt tips were to keep the boys from getting hurt."

"Forevermore!" Miss Pickerell gasped.

"Yes, indeed," Professor Tuttle said. "Our first finds, the purple glass, the snuffbox, the rusty hinge, the toothpick—all of those were from the colonial period. We're digging into the Indian times, now. Mr. Esticott, why don't you take Miss Pickerell into the test pit and show her where we made our discoveries? In the meantime, I'll sort out some of these finds for possible dating."

Mr. Esticott turned to Miss Pickerell. "You'll have to climb down a ladder to get inside now," he told her. "We've dug pretty deep."

"I'm not afraid of ladders," Miss Pickerell replied, unabashed.

She followed Mr. Esticott into the pit. It had been dug so deep, it looked like a tunnel now. Mr. Esticott led her farther and farther inside.

"It's like a house with different rooms in it," Mr. Esticott said. "This is the part where we found the doll and the cradle board and the blunt-tipped arrows."

"Mercy!" Miss Pickerell breathed.

Mr. Esticott walked on a little farther.

"And this is the place where we unearthed the bowls and the spoons and the ladles," he told her.

"Maybe it was a kitchen," Miss Pickerell said. "Or even a dining room. That is, if they had dining rooms in those days."

"And here," Mr. Esticott said, moving on quickly and motioning for her to join him, "here is where . . ."

The sound of stones falling and the sudden, choking smell of heavy dust, rapidly accumulating, came before Mr. Esticott had a chance to finish.

Miss Pickerell staggered forward. "What . . . what . . ." she asked, trying hard to talk through the dust that was sweeping around her.

"The shoring." Mr. Esticott's voice spoke from sudden darkness beside her. "I think it has caved in."

CHAPTER TEN

Cave-In

Miss Pickerell groped blindly. Right in front of her was what seemed to be a short wall, extending up only to her chin. It felt solid. She got down on her hands and knees next to it, and reached out a hand toward Mr. Esticott, pulling him down with her.

Suddenly all was quiet. Miss Pickerell could hear the sound of her own heart beating, and Mr. Esticott's quick, heavy breathing.

"Mr. Esticott!" she whispered. "Are you all right?"

"Yes," he replied, "except for this dust which has gotten up into my nose. I can't . . ."

"Do you have a flashlight?" Miss Pickerell interrupted.

"In my back pocket," Mr. Esticott said. "I'll get it."

The flashlight was small. When Mr. Esticott held it out, Miss Pickerell could just barely see what had happened. The wooden boards used as shoring on the right side of the pit had com-

pletely collapsed. With them had fallen stones
and hard-packed clumps of earth. The ladder,
which had been pushed by the impact into an
uncertain horizontal position, was covered with
rocks and boards. The opening out of the pit
was solidly blocked.

In the flashlight's beam, Miss Pickerell caught
a glimpse of Mr. Esticott's face. His eyes were
full of fear.

"We're trapped," he said shakily. "Sealed
in!"

"Stop talking that way," Miss Pickerell said,
hoping she sounded firm enough. "There must
be a way out."

"Where?" Mr. Esticott asked.

"I don't know yet," Miss Pickerell said.
"But I plan to find out. Let me have that
flashlight, please."

"Mr. Esticott handed over the flashlight re-
luctantly. "I don't think you ought to poke
around too much, Miss Pickerell," he cau-
tioned. "It might be dangerous. You could be
upsetting something that would start another
avalanche."

Miss Pickerell thought about this.

"You may be right," she said, sighing.

"They know outside the pit that the shoring
has caved in," Mr. Esticott went on, talking

more confidently now. "They're bound to come and rescue us."

"Yes," Miss Pickerell said. She tried hard to be patient and wait. It was very difficult. Minutes passed. There was no sign of movement from outside. And the air inside was getting more suffocating by the second.

"I can't bear it," Miss Pickerell said finally. "I can't bear just sitting here and doing nothing. There must be *something* we can do to help ourselves."

"What?" Mr. Esticott asked, sounding desperate.

"Look for another way out," Miss Pickerell said, resolutely holding the flashlight out in front of her.

Both Miss Pickerell and Mr. Esticott saw the opening at the same instant. It was at the right, not too far from where the lower part of the wall ended. The crash of timber and stones had rolled away some of the earth there, revealing a hole just large enough to crawl through.

"Where do you suppose it leads?" Mr. Esticott asked breathlessly.

"We'll soon know," Miss Pickerell said.

Clutching the flashlight in one hand and Mr. Esticott's arm with the other, she began moving in the direction of the opening. It was hard to move quickly. The ground was rough and rocky and every once in a while she or Mr. Esticott came close to falling.

When they reached the hole, Miss Pickerell crawled through first. Mr. Esticott followed immediately.

What they saw made them both gasp. They were in what seemed to be a small room, shaped like an upside-down cup. And lying so near to the entrance that they almost stumbled over it, was a pile of what looked very much like weapons. Miss Pickerell turned the flashlight full on them.

"Spearheads!" Mr. Esticott exclaimed, pointing to those first.

"Arrowheads!" Miss Pickerell said, noticing these next. "Stone-tipped arrowheads."

"I've seen pictures of them in the new dictionary my cousin sent me last year," Mr. Esticott said. "In the A section."

"They're also likely to be in the F section," Miss Pickerell added. "Under FLINT. Both spearpoints and arrowheads were often made of hard flint stone. Professor Tuttle will be most interested in what we've found."

"Yes, *when* we're able to get out and tell him about it," Mr. Esticott replied.

"We'll get out soon," Miss Pickerell said, trying to feel optimistic. "We might even find an exit leading out from this room. Let's walk all around it."

Once again, holding the flashlight in front of her, she began to creep carefully forward. Mr. Esticott followed, almost in her footsteps. When she had gone far enough to be able to touch a wall of the vaultlike chamber, she stopped and deliberately dropped her bright white handkerchief. "So that we'll know where we started from," she said.

They continued to grope their way around the curve of the room. Miss Pickerell kept swinging the flashlight upward and downward in a series of slow arcs. Mr. Esticott fumbled all along the clay-packed walls for an opening. There was none.

"Let's try the ground," Mr. Esticott suggested when they were back at the spot marked by the handkerchief. "Perhaps there's a tunnel leading out from underneath."

Miss Pickerell did not answer. She was staring at something on the wall. "Here's a spot we must have missed," she said.

Mr. Esticott moved over to where she stood and stared too.

Built into the wall quite near the ground was what seemed to be a crude fireplace. And in

and around this hearth were set a number of interestingly shaped stones, each bearing a pattern of regular ridges, and with a slightly hollowed-out center. The rocks were black with soot.

"Why, it looks like a fireplace—doesn't it?" exclaimed Mr. Esticott.

"It most certainly does, Mr. Esticott," Miss Pickerell replied. "But there's something about those rocks! Something strange. I'm taking one of them back with me!"

She leaned down and pulled until she had loosened one of the rocks. She examined it thoughtfully. Then she put it in her apron pocket. "I know what these rocks remind me of!" she said at last. "I know, but I don't understand it at all."

CHAPTER ELEVEN

A Sign from the Rescuers

Miss Pickerell and Mr. Esticott stood now in almost total blackness. The flashlight was flickering badly.

"We'd better put it out," Miss Pickerell suggested. "Unless you have an extra battery with you."

"I haven't," Mr. Esticott sighed. "What do we do now?"

"First we'll go back and wait," Miss Pickerell said. "We'd better get back to where we started from, before your flashlight goes dead. It's certainly time the rescuers were getting down to us!"

When Miss Pickerell and Mr. Esticott had crawled back through the hole and were once more seated on the uneven ground near the low wall, Miss Pickerell took one last look around. "Let's get our bearings," she said firmly. "We're between the wall and the left-hand side of the pit. The rescuers will most probably come from the left side because that's the part where the shoring is still fairly intact. What do you think, Mr. Esticott?"

"I think so, too," he said.

"We'll listen for sounds from that direction," Miss Pickerell said, accompanying her words with a brisk snap of the "off" switch. "We'll turn the flashlight on every fifteen minutes or so to look for signs of movement."

Mr. Esticott had nothing to say.

Miss Pickerell tried to think of something to talk about that might make them feel better. "Just imagine, Mr. Esticott," she said, "hundreds and hundreds of years ago a family lived in that strange-shaped room, and a mother cooked dinner in that very fireplace."

"Is there any way we can tell exactly when that was?" Mr. Esticott asked.

Miss Pickerell reached into her pocket and pulled out the rock. She turned the flashlight on it briefly. "The answer is in the carbon soot on this rock, Mr. Esticott," she said. "The soot is all that's left of a piece of wood that was burned in that fireplace. If we can tell how old the soot is, we'll know when people used the fireplace!"

"But how can we tell how old the soot is?" Mr. Esticott asked bewildered.

"Wait! Sh!" Miss Pickerell hissed sharply.

A tiny scratching noise seemed to be coming from somewhere up above. Miss Pickerell turned on the flashlight immediately. But she saw nothing. And the sound was not repeated.

Mr. Esticott sighed. "What were you saying about dating soot?" he asked.

"I was going to tell you about the carbon-14 test," Miss Pickerell answered. "I learned about it once when I was helping someone look for uranium. It's a scientific way of dating things that were once alive."

"I don't see how that has anything to do with soot," Mr. Esticott said sounding doubtful.

"It's really very simple," Miss Pickerell told him. "The soot on this rock was formed when wood was burned in that fireplace. And the wood came from a living tree. Of course, every living thing contains radioactive carbon-14, because carbon-14 is in the air. For example, plants take it in."

Miss Pickerell stopped suddenly. Again, it seemed to her that she heard small sounds above her. Again, there was nothing when she strained her ears to listen and when she turned the flashlight on to look. She sighed heavily.

"After a plant dies," she resumed, "the carbon-14 disintegrates at a *known* rate, a certain amount every year. If we can get a scientist to measure how much carbon-14 is left in this soot, we'll have a very good idea of its age."

"Oh!" Mr. Esticott said.

Miss Pickerell said nothing more. She felt tired after her long speech. It was becoming harder and harder to breathe in the close atmosphere. She was also very thirsty. She searched in her knitting bag for the peppermint candy drops she usually carried there. She found two. Mr. Esticott gladly accepted one when she offered it to him.

She was just taking the wrapper off her own piece when she thought she heard noises again. This time, they sounded louder and seemed definitely to come from the left side of the pit. Miss Pickerell turned the flashlight on.

"Maybe they're tapping," she said. "I'm going to tap back."

"Why not shout?" Mr. Esticott asked and began immediately, "Hello! We're here!"

Miss Pickerell joined him. "Hello! Right here!"

No one answered.

"I'll try tapping against the shoring," Miss Pickerell said, picking up a rock from the ground. "I'll tap with this."

Miss Pickerell tapped systematically. Once, twice, three times—four times. Almost immediately, a trickle of earth began to sift down, and quickly broadened into a stream that poured

102

and then surged toward her and Mr. Esticott.

"Oh!" Miss Pickerell gasped, not certain whether to jump back or to crouch down. "They must have heard the tapping. They know where we are now."

"I see something coming through!" Mr. Esticott cried out.

A dark, round object poked out of the earth above their heads. Slowly, the object thrust out farther and farther.

Miss Pickerell kept the dimmed flashlight fixed in that direction and peered anxiously. "Forevermore!" she blurted out in astonishment.

"What is it?" Mr. Esticott asked. "What is it?"

"It's a drainpipe," said Miss Pickerell, feeling very awed and trying hard to keep her voice steady. "The rescuers are pushing it through to make contact with us."

When the pipe stopped moving, Miss Pickerell approached it. She stood on tiptoe, her eye just reaching the level of the hollow end. She took time only to wipe off the right lens of her eyeglasses, then squinted cautiously up the length of the pipe. "I see daylight!" she shouted.

"Hooray!" yelled Mr. Esticott. "May I look, too?"

Miss Pickerell stepped away.

Mr. Esticott, cupping his hands around the end of the pipe and craning his neck as far as it would go, stared hard. "I see a little circle of daylight at the other end!" he announced. "And I think I see someone moving around up there!"

"We'll have to let them know that they have reached us," said Miss Pickerell. "We must attend to that at once."

CHAPTER TWELVE

"Light, We Need Light!"

Miss Pickerell knew immediately what she had to do. She pursed her lips up as if she were about to whistle, pressed them hard against the hollow end of the drainpipe, and, making her voice as loud as she could, called out, "YOO HOO! YOO HOO!"

The muffled answer came back instantly, "Can you hear us?"

"Yes!" Miss Pickerell shouted.

"Are you all right?" the voice, which Miss Pickerell was beginning to distinguish as Professor Tuttle's, asked.

"We're both fine," Miss Pickerell answered.

"Good," the answer came. "We're digging down to you. We're coming straight through about a yard to the left of this pipe. Stay as far away from there as possible. It may be dangerous. Do you understand?"

"Yes," Miss Pickerell said, impressed by the urgency in Professor Tuttle's voice.

"One last thing," the professor called. "We have to shore up the top of this pit as we keep digging. It may take us a while. Don't be frightened."

"I won't," Miss Pickerell said. "Thank you, Professor."

She sighed with relief and turned to Mr. Esticott. "I guess our troubles are over now," she said.

At that precise moment, the flashlight went dead. Miss Pickerell could not see even an inch in front of her.

"This is the last straw," Mr. Esticott burst out.

"That may be," Miss Pickerell agreed, "but I don't intend to sit here in the dark until we're rescued." She reached for the pipe again and shouted up to the diggers, "Light, we need light!"

Mr. Esticott cleared his throat. "Do you think that will help?" he asked.

"I wouldn't have done it otherwise," Miss Pickerell replied in very definite tones.

"What did you say?" Mr. Esticott asked.

Miss Pickerell was not surprised that he hadn't heard her. Something was loudly clanking its way down the drainpipe. It came to a halt at the very end of the pipe. It was a flashlight and it was lit.

"Why, it's Euphus' new silver flash!" Miss Pickerell exclaimed. "I bought it for him myself on his last birthday. He must have gotten my message."

"Look," Mr. Esticott said, showing her how the flashlight was tied on to a piece of wool. It was the green knitting wool that she had given to Mr. Humwhistel when he was attaching labels to the finds.

"Of course," Miss Pickerell replied. "That's the way Euphus lowered the flash through the pipe. If he'd just thrown it down, it would have fallen right out at the end and broken to bits."

"You have a very smart nephew," Mr. Esticott said admiringly.

"All seven of my nephews and nieces are smart," Miss Pickerell replied proudly. "Each in a different way."

Now that they had some light, Miss Pickerell and Mr. Esticott felt considerably more cheerful. They felt even better when the first whiffs of fresh air began to drift down into the trench. Miss Pickerell stopped to draw in long, deep breaths. Mr. Esticott did the same.

"It shouldn't be long now," he said happily.

"I don't imagine it should," Miss Pickerell agreed.

They had nothing to do now but wait. Miss Pickerell thought about Professor Tuttle's old, old rock from far, far away, and about the strange cup-shaped room. And suddenly something fell into place in her mind. "Mr. Esticott," she said, "I've been thinking. Houses are like children. They resemble their parents."

"I beg your pardon?" Mr. Esticott said, looking quite bewildered.

Miss Pickerell tried hard to explain. To her, it all seemed so clear. "What I'm trying to tell you, Mr. Esticott," she said, "is that this rock in my pocket closely resembles a rock that Professor Tuttle showed me when I met him the other day. But his rock came from another continent, and was centuries old." She stopped suddenly, as the idea came to her. "Could it be," she said a few seconds later, "that the descendants of the people who fashioned Professor Tuttle's rock once lived in Square Toe County?"

Mr. Esticott stared, open-mouthed.

"Yes," Miss Pickerell continued, hardly able to contain her excitement. "That's why we see the same workmanship. Square Toe County may have a past we never even dreamed existed. We may learn who . . ."

But Mr. Esticott was no longer listening to her. He was looking up at the top of the pit. A noisy downflow of earth had suddenly opened up a large hole, revealing first a shovel, then a hand, and, at last, Mr. Rugby's round, shining face, peering down at them and smiling broadly.

CHAPTER THIRTEEN

A Clue to the Past

"If you'll just step over that rubble, Miss Pickerell," Mr. Rugby said, pointing to the place where the ladder had fallen, and cheerfully extending a hand for her to grasp, "I'll help you out of the pit."

"Thank you, Mr. Rugby," Miss Pickerell said, feeling more confident when she noticed that Mr. Humwhistel stood behind Mr. Rugby, hands tightly clasped around Mr. Rugby's waist and legs firmly balanced on the ground.

"Go ahead, Miss Pickerell," Mr. Esticott said. "I'll be right behind you, in case you slip."

"I have no intention of slipping," Miss Pickerell told him, as she made her way over the ladder and reached out for Mr. Rugby's hand.

"One—two—three—UP!" Mr. Rugby said, supporting her while she tried to climb toward him. Mr. Esticott followed.

Once out in the open, in the late afternoon sunshine, it wasn't very hard to forget the darkness and the terror of the caved-in trench. And after Miss Pickerell had had two glasses of peppermintade, made for her by the Scouts un-

110

"One—two—three—UP!"

der Mr. Rugby's supervision, and eaten half a cheese sandwich that Mr. Humwhistel offered her, she was as ready as ever for action.

But first she had one question. Why had the shoring collapsed? Miss Pickerell put the question to Professor Tuttle, who was hovering around anxiously.

"Rain, rain!" muttered the professor. "It plagues archeologists the world over, and softens the earth in our excavations. And then there were all those spectators—it's no wonder there was a cave-in!"

Miss Pickerell nodded her understanding. "I think I can tell you something interesting about your rock, Professor Tuttle," she said.

"Yes?" Professor Tuttle asked.

Miss Pickerell tried hard to sort out the ideas that were racing around in her head. She knew she would have to explain them clearly if she wanted Professor Tuttle to understand.

"Yes?" Professor Tuttle asked again.

"Well," Miss Pickerell said, adjusting a hairpin that had suddenly come loose, and speaking slowly and carefully, "I found a rock that seems to have exactly the same workmanship as the rock you showed me—the one you left in Mr. Rugby's storeroom."

"My rock!" Professor Tuttle exclaimed.

"My rock that Professor Temerdekoff sent me from Siberia?"

"What is even more important," Miss Pickerell went on calmly, "is that this rock I found is full of soot. It was part of a primitive kind of fireplace that Mr. Esticott and I discovered while we were trapped down there. And, as I said to Mr. Esticott, we can date this soot with the carbon-14 test."

Professor Tuttle stared. "Do you realize what you're saying, Miss Pickerell?" he asked in an unbelieving tone of voice. "Do you know that if the carbon-14 test shows that the soot on your rock is very, very old—perhaps ten or even fifty thousand years old—it may mean that the people who fashioned my rock, or their children or grandchildren or great-grandchildren once lived in North America? That would explain the strange similarities between the markings on the two rocks."

"That's just what I had in mind," Miss Pickerell said, feeling relieved that she had made herself clear to the professor, and taking the rock out of her apron pocket to give him.

The professor took it immediately. "Miss Pickerell," he said, looking at her with open admiration, "you may be helping us to rewrite the pages of our American history books. You may be making it possible for us to learn when the first people came to this continent, and where they came from."

Miss Pickerell felt doubtful. "Yes," she said, "but if they came from another continent, like Asia, how did they get here?"

"We believe they must have walked over a land bridge that once existed between Siberia and Alaska—now it's ocean, the Bering Straits." Professor Tuttle explained.

"Goodness!" Miss Pickerell said, remembering that her nephew, Euphus, had once told her something about studying this theory of early migration from Asia to the North American continent. But she felt too tired to ask how a land bridge could spring up in the middle of an ocean and then disappear again. She felt a strange kind of tiredness mixed up suddenly with memories of the musty smells in the pit.

Mr. Rugby noticed it first. "You look a little pale, Miss Pickerell," he said sounding worried.

"Would you like me to drive you home?" Mr. Humwhistel asked.

"Not at all," Miss Pickerell replied. "I probably need some rest. But I can drive myself home."

She felt very silly walking up the slope. She consoled herself with the thought that she knew very few people who would not feel dizzy and exhausted after so many hours spent in a cave-in. As she looked across the mountains and watched the sun quietly setting in the distance, Miss Pickerell knew that the frightening memories would soon go away. There was much too much to be happy about to bother with such nonsense.

CHAPTER FOURTEEN

Testing

Miss Pickerell returned to the pit with renewed vigor the next morning. Everybody was busy digging, dusting, recording, and photographing. Mr. Esticott, working nearest the pit opening, said that Professor Tuttle was in a bad mood because he still hadn't been able to make contact with the laboratory for carbon-14 testing. He was at Mr. Rugby's diner right now, trying again. Mr. Rugby, who saw her, too, pointed to a camp stool, set up near the opening. "I brought it for you," he explained. "From Mr. Kettelson's store."

Don't worry about me," Miss Pickerell said. "What can I do?"

"Sit down for the time being," Mr. Esticott said. "We're finding so many new things. I'm sure Professor Tuttle will be pleased."

"Will you keep me informed about them?" Miss Pickerell asked.

Both men promised to do this. Mr. Rugby leaned out after each discovery and relayed the description that Mr. Humwhistel, farther down in the pit, was dictating for Euphus to record.

To keep Miss Pickerell absolutely up to date, he interspersed each description with comments of his own: "One drum, made out of a hollowed-out log; Mr. Humwhistel says a sample from this can also be submitted for carbon-14 testing. One toy loom with a wooden frame; ditto about the wooden frame. One hoop made of strings knotted together; Mr. Humwhistel says this was for arrow practice, but I don't know what he means. Two birch-bark lollipops; the bark is rolled into the shape of a cone and Mr. Humwhistel says the mothers used to fill these with snow and then pour maple syrup over the snow. Maybe the children had them for dessert. I'm not sure."

Miss Pickerell half-closed her eyes. It was almost like being in a dream, she told herself, watching the past come alive, object by object. These children probably begged for birch-bark lollipops the way her own young nieces and nephews pleaded for candy or ice cream. And the older people probably wondered, exactly the way she did, how children could eat so much sweet stuff and not get sick.

She came to with a start when she saw the Scouts marching out of the pit. Mr. Humwhistel was sending them home.

"I promised your mothers I'd send you back

early today," he said. "Besides, we're not going to do any more work in the pit now."

"What about tomorrow . . . what about the bulldozer . . . what about more digging tomorrow?" the Scouts clamored, as Mr. Humwhistel tried to answer them and to get them to leave.

"Most likely, he doesn't know what to tell them," Miss Pickerell said to herself. "I hardly know, either."

Mr. Esticott was climbing out of the pit now. "I've been put in charge of wrapping," he said. "Professor Tuttle announced that we'd take the finds to the laboratory and just stand outside the door until someone arrives, if there is no other way."

"Mr. Rugby!" Professor Tuttle shouted, appearing suddenly in their midst and waving a piece of paper. "You were so busy talking, you never even saw me come back. I've finally reached the laboratory at the university. I knew they were open on Sunday! Here are the road directions. Just follow the road numbers that I've indicated. The man at the laboratory says this is the fastest way to get there."

"Why, they're exactly like my short cut!" Mr. Rugby exclaimed, when he examined the directions.

"And now, Mr. Esticott, on with the wrapping, please," Professor Tuttle went on. "As carefully as you can."

"In my job as baggage master," Mr. Esticott said a little coldly, "I am often called on to do delicate wrapping."

Mr. Humwhistel handed each find separately to Mr. Esticott. Mr. Esticott wrapped it in tissue-lined newspaper and placed it, cradled in some more newspaper, in a large basket. Mr. Rugby transferred the basket to the back of his station wagon, hedging it around with cartons so that it wouldn't slide.

"How long does this carbon-14 testing take?" Miss Pickerell asked when everything was finally settled and Mr. Rugby was ready to go.

"Handled as an emergency, twelve to fourteen hours," Professor Tuttle replied. "They have a long waiting list for the carbon-14 test at the university laboratory. But the chief is a friend of mine. He's the man I was on my way to visit when that train delay kept me in Square Toe City. I was going to present him with my rock. He knows how important these finds are and he's very sorry he couldn't be reached until . . ."

"Twelve to fourteen hours!" Miss Pickerell interrupted impatiently. "And at least six hours for traveling back and forth. Why it will be seven o'clock in the morning by the time you return. The bulldozer will be here."

"The bulldozer won't do any more damage here, if we learn that these finds are important," Professor Tuttle said. "If we authenticate my hunch that these finds go back to long before Columbus' time, the state will be only too anxious for us to keep on digging! Square Toe County will become famous as the first . . ."

"What if you're late in coming back?" Miss Pickerell interrupted again. "What if you're late and the bulldozer is here?"

She answered her own question. "I'll sleep here," she said. "I'll stay right here on this camp stool. I'll be right on the spot and I'll see to it that the bulldozer doesn't start working."

"Hooray!" Mr. Rugby shouted.

"Bravo!" Professor Tuttle said.

"Wonderful!" Mr. Humwhistel said, looking questioningly at Mr. Esticott and Professor Tuttle, each of whom nodded his head in agreement. "We'll all stay here with you," they said.

CHAPTER FIFTEEN

Honorary Indians

Miss Pickerell awoke to a confusion of noises. The bulldozer on the hill was grinding its gears into action. It seemed to be doing this in accompaniment to a steady whirring sound above. Miss Pickerell looked up. A helicopter was racing across the sky, flying lower and lower, preparing for its descent. Miss Pickerell closed her eyes and put her hands over her ears just before the helicopter swept down and landed on the highway, in the path of the bulldozer. The three men standing around her said, "It's all right, Miss Pickerell."

She opened her eyes to see the Governor getting out of the helicopter. With him were Mr. Rugby and a man and a woman she did not recognize. Professor Tuttle told her that the man was his friend from the state university laboratory. The woman, who wore a flowered dress and a big straw picture hat, came over and introduced herself as the feature reporter from the *Square Toe Gazette*. She had come, at the Governor's suggestion, she explained, for a personal interview with Miss Pickerell.

Miss Pickerell had no chance to say anything. The sheriff's car came screeching up the road. He stopped alongside the helicopter, walked over to the bulldozer, and flashing his badge, said, "Stop, in the name of the law!"

Mr. Gilhuly's mail truck came next. "I told you I'd be able to locate him, Governor," Mr. Gilhuly said, as he escorted a very erect-looking man out of the truck. The man wore an Indian shawl on his shoulders and had two long black braids hanging down his back.

Then came a television truck and a truck with a movie camera; and Dwight, Miss Pickerell's oldest nephew, driving his car and bringing Rosemary and Euphus and Mr. Butterworth; and Mr. Kettleson, in a station wagon, bringing the rest of her seven nieces and nephews and their parents; and Boy Scouts and Girl Scouts and their parents, on foot and in cars.

"I alerted them all," Mr. Rugby announced proudly, from where he was standing just behind the Governor. The Governor was shaking Miss Pickerell's hand up and down vigorously. "The soot on that rock you took out of the wall, Miss Pickerell," Professor Tuttle's friend from the state university laboratory came up to tell her, "goes back approximately eleven thousand years. It is my opinion that if we keep on

122

digging, we'll make discoveries that go back even further."

"And keep on digging, we will," the Governor said. "As long as we have to. The widening of the road can wait."

The man with the braids walked up to Miss Pickerell. "My name is Chief Stout Heart," he said. "I want to tell everybody how much these finds mean to me. Some of us Indians have always believed that we were descended from the people who first came over to America from Asia, thousands and thousands of years ago, before the great glaciers moved over the land and separated the continents by water."

Miss Pickerell said, "Oh!" She turned to Professor Tuttle. "Is that what you meant," she asked, "when you said that the ancestors of the American Indians might have come across a land bridge that no longer exists?"

"I certainly did," Professor Tuttle said. "As Chief Stout Heart was saying, during the Ice Age, great glaciers grew up and moved over the land. They accumulated so much ocean water that the sea level got lower and lower. That's how the land bridge came into being. But then, later, the water in the glaciers melted and the land bridge was covered over."

"That's what I thought," Chief Stout Heart

went on. "And now, Miss Pickerell, we would like to show our appreciation to you, and of course to you, Professor Tuttle, and to you, Mr. Humwhistle, Mr. Rugby, and Mr. Esticott, by inviting you to become honorary members of our tribe."

Everybody cheered, the children loudest of all. Professor Tuttle, Mr. Humwhistel, Mr. Rugby and Mr. Esticott shook hands with Chief

Stout Heart and murmured their thanks.

Miss Pickerell felt very touched. She also wondered why Chief Stout Heart had not mentioned the Scouts. "Thank you very much," she said, trying to make herself heard in all the excitement. "But what about the Scouts? They worked so hard with . . ."

"I have not forgotten the Scouts," Chief Stout Heart announced. "I am presenting each of them with an authentic Indian headdress."

"Oh!" the children screamed happily.

The lady reporter with the big straw picture

hat came back from wandering in the crowd to talk to Miss Pickerell. "How does it feel to be always in the forefront of scientific adventures?" she asked Miss Pickerell.

Miss Pickerell reflected before answering. "It's most exciting when the adventure is happening," she said. "But in between adventures, I'm just as happy when I'm home with my cow and my cat."

The lady reporter copied the words down carefully so that they could be printed exactly the way Miss Pickerell had said them in the next day's newspaper.

About the Authors and the Artist

ELLEN MAC GREGOR'S books for children have won her countless devoted fans throughout the country and abroad. *Mr. Ferguson of the Fire Department* and *Theodore Turtle*, her picture books with Paul Galdone's illustrations, continue to be popular.

Then Miss Pickerell was created, and became an immediate success. Each of the four adventures brought hundreds of demands for more Miss Pickerell stories. Ellen MacGregor left boxes of notes and plans for future Miss Pickerell adventures, and although several writers tried, Dora Pantell is the first to capture Miss Pickerell's unique personality. Now, that spunky heroine is back, in *Miss Pickerell on the Moon* and in *Miss Pickerell Goes on a Dig*. Backed, as usual, with up-to-date scientific concepts, these fresh adventures present beloved Ellen MacGregor characters and delightful new ones in plots created by Dora Pantell.

DORA PANTELL has taught adults and children of all ages, and has written for various publications and for radio and television—in addition to appearing on television to demonstrate teaching techniques. She is a curriculum consultant for the New York City Board of Education, writing and evaluating curriculum programs and actual reading matter for use in the teaching of English as a second language. Miss Pantell has also written material for the federal government's anti-poverty program.

CHARLES GEER is a graduate of Pratt Institute, and has been a popular illustrator of children's books for over fifteen years.